EROTICA

JEWEL ALYSSA

Erotic/Romance

Cover image: Pixabay.com

Cover Design: HRK

This is a work of fiction. Names, places, incidents and characters are the product of the author's imagination or used in a fictitious manner. Any resemblance to actual persons, living or dead is entirely coincidental.

No part of this book may be reproduced, distributed or transmitted in any form or by any means including photocopying recording or any other methods without the permission of the author.

Author can be reached by mail.

Jewelalyssa93writer@gmail.com

<u>**WARNING 18+**</u>

This book contains mature content, explicit erotic scenes and language.

Table of contents

1. The neighbor . . . 07
2. Virgin predator . . 17
3. Intentions . . . 31
4. Sexual fever . . . 39
5. My wife's sister . . 49
6. Desperations . . . 57
7. The girl next door . . 67
8. Carnal desires . . . 77
9. My hot neighbor . . 97
10. Invitation . . . 115

<u>Top stories by Jewel Alyssa</u>

Widow's Desire

The Snake Goddess

The seduced

Sex is serene

The sorcerer 1

The sorcerer 2

The sorcerer 3

Lust is divine

Blue 1: Abused

Blue 2: Locked

The neighbor

My name is Rohan. I am twenty. I study in college for B.Com.

My family was very close with our neighbors. Their family has migrated from somewhere in the north and has been living in our neighborhood for last three years.

I was having vacation for summer holidays and was enjoying my time of freedom.

One day the neighbor aunty came to our house for an unusual request.

Her mother in law was admitted in a hospital and her husband was staying back at the hospital. The hospital was far away, somewhere in the northern states.

The daily up and down was not possible. She and her kids were alone at home and they needed someone to be with them.

She requested my mom to send me with them to stay at night at their house.

My mom couldn't deny her request.

She called me and said. "Rohan, you are having a vacation. So you should stay at her house at night. Uncle is far away and they are feeling unprotected. It is our duty to keep them feels secure."

I didn't have a choice.

Let me introduce the aunty now.

Her name is Subha. She is thirty three. She is around 5 foot 3. Her skin was a little tanned, black hair and had a plump body. She had big breasts and back.

I would admit I have jerked off thinking about her a lot of times.

She was an amazing lady, sexy to be honest. Even the sight of her would make my cock hard.

She has two kids, both girls. One is 8 and the other is 5. Maybe because of that she liked me.

I had freedom in that house. She used to call me if she needed to buy groceries and other stuff, even sanitary napkins for her.

Subha looked at me and smiled. "Have dinner with us tonight." she invited.

I looked at my mom. She neither supported nor opposed leaving me confused. I waited for a few more minutes for her to say something but she doesn't even notice me.

Mom and Subha started talking about her mother in law and her illness. I decided to leave them alone.

At 7 in the evening my mom called me and said.

"It is better if you go there before dark."

"Ok mom."

"Have your supper there. She may have made something for you. Don't be greedy and eat slowly." She smirked.

I changed into my night dress, a loose pajamas and vest. I was wearing nothing under the pajamas. I am sure I would be sleeping in the hall.

Their house had only two bedrooms. In one of them Subha and her husband would be sleeping and the other would be the kids bedroom.

I reached their home gleefully. I was happy that I would be able to stare at her, watch her for hours with my stealthy eyes.

The kids were also happy to see me. We played card games and board games. How the time went, we never knew. At 9, Subha called us for dinner.

She served dinner and while serving her big tits wriggled against my back. Though it happened unknowingly my prick was hard in a moment.

After dinner the children went to sleep in their room and I sat at the hall watching TV.

The hall room had four chairs but no couch. I thought I would have to sleep on the floor. *Fuck that.*

Subha finished her dinner and came to the hall and asked me. "Are you sleepy?"

"Yes aunty." I said.

"Come with me." she instructed and walked away. I followed her and we reached their bedroom.

"We don't have an extra bedroom. So you can sleep here."

"Give me a bed sheet and a pillow." I said.

"Why a bed sheet and pillow?" she was surprised.

"I will sleep on the floor." I replied.

She shook her head. "Sleeping on the cold floor will give you back ache in the morning. Sleep with me in the bed." her voice was solid but tempting.

My heart was filled with joy.

I dreamt of touching her in the sleep, caressing her big melons and feeling the heat of her thick cunt.

My rod was getting hard and tried to hide it with my hands.

I quickly lay on my stomach so that she won't see my cock aroused.

I heard the bathroom door getting closed.

After a few seconds she came back wearing a smooth silky night gown.

I saw her hard nipples. Uff, my rod was erect again. At that moment I knew my rod will be hard all night.

She switched the lights off and lay beside me. Few moments later I knew she was asleep.

I slide closer to her so there was hardly a little gap remained between us. She was on her back. I lay sideways facing towards her, my hard cock too close to her hips.

It was a full moon night and the moonlight came through the window. I could see her chest rising with each breath she took.

I wanted to grab them, bite those nipples and nibble all over her big breasts all night.

She twitched in her sleep towards me. Her tits pressed against my chest, her thighs touching my throbbing cock and her hand around me. My cock was vibrating on her thighs and I couldn't move back.

She wasn't wearing any bra inside. Her breasts were loose and squeezed against me. My heart was thumping inside.

Now I could feel her hand sliding down from my back and grabbing my cock.

I gasped for a moment. It was the first time someone holding my cock.

Suddenly she jumped up and switched on the table lamp. She saw me; my eyes open wide and staring at her.

"I...I" she stuttered. "I thought it was my husband. I am sorry." She apologized.

I was also voiceless but I managed to reply her. "It's ok. I also thought so."

My voice made her relax. "Do you have a girlfriend?"

Shyly I replied, no.

She leaned onto the bed again closer to me. I can feel her warm breath hitting on my face. She was horny, I knew.

I kept my hand on her shoulder. She didn't resist. I moved closer and let my cock touch her thighs. Again she seemed unperturbed.

I slid my hand and kept on her melon and nibbled her nipple with my thumb.

A soft moan escaped her mouth. That was encouraging.

"Can I?" she asked. But before she completed my cock was inside her fist. She held it forcibly, feeling the hardness of my rod. As her pressure increased I gripped her melon hard.

We both groaned at the same time.

I kissed her and she opened her mouth to let my tongue enter. I let her suck my tongue.

Now I was over her, my both hands squeezing each of her breasts.

She pushed me and asked me to undress. While I did she removed her maxi revealing her plump body.

I saw her thick cunt lips, big breasts, hard aroused nipples and curvy belly.

I was all heated up now. My cock was really hard even ready to pierce through any metal.

I sucked her nipples and nibbled around her tits with my tongue. I kissed her all over her body.

We were on bed again when I tongued her belly button. She writhed with pleasure.

She pushed me down till my head was between her legs; my tongue was over her clit.

I can smell her pussy, a mesmerizing odor coming from her cunt slowly blinding my senses.

This was my first time of having a chance to smell a cunt.

I badly wanted to feel the insides of a cunt and I inserted my finger inside her.

It was heavenly soft and wet. I pushed my finger in and out smoothly. I added another one.

Sweet moans came out of Subha's mouth. She opened her legs wide for me.

I took out my wet fingers. They were covered with translucent white fluid. The aroma was all around me now. I was being hypnotized by the fragrance of her cunt juice.

I started licking her wet cunt and felt her cunt honey on my tongue. It felt ecstatic.

She lifted her ass for me and my tongue trailed down to her butt hole.

After a while, she pushed me down to the bed and started stroking my cock.

"This is good. This is better than my husband." She whispered.

She took my hard muscle in her mouth till its end touch her throat. She stroked it with her mouth and it felt like heaven.

She climbed on top of me and rubbed her moist cunt on my cock. Then she slid it inside her pussy and started pushing it in and out gently.

It went inside her smoothly as her cunt was leaking lots of honey.

We both gasped and moaned at the same time.

Her hips movements became fast and the sound of her butt cheeks hitting my groin filled the room.

I squashed her tits with my hands and nibbled with my fingers.

Then she asked me to be on top and do the work. We changed positions. I was on top now.

She guided my cock into her cunt. I forced my wood hardly into her pussy. I felt my cock rubbing her cunt walls. She was all wet and heated up. Her cunt honey was drooling out.

She held my butt cheeks and controlled my speed of action.

I wasn't stopping; my cock entered her cunt and exited in rhythm with full force hitting her womb with a pleasurable tempo.

She moaned and groaned uncontrollably.

Her voices filled the room and it made me more enthusiastic. I hit her womb hard with all my strength.

I filled her cunt with my cream. I thrusted again and again till the last drop of my cream was inside her.

I lay on top of her squeezing her tits under my chest with my cock still inside her cunt.

She kissed me with passion.

Her hands squashed my butt and she inserted one finger in my ass hole. She moved her finger in and out which gave me an unimaginable pleasure.

She was still moaning and she inserted one more finger into my butthole. Two fingers were too tight. I felt a little pain but I didn't mind. I let her do whatever she would like to do.

She pushed my ass gently so my soft cock still moves inside her cunt.

"Can you fuck me again?" she asked. "I want more."

"My cock is now soft." I said. "Let me clean it. And you can suck it and make it hard."

"There is no need of cleaning. Just give it in my mouth."

"But it is covered with my creamy milk."

"I will happily taste and swallow it."

I removed my cock from her cunt. As it was out I saw loads of cum running down her pussy.

I took the cum in my hands and poured it into her mouth.

"Have my cum."

She swallowed happily.

I, then put my cum covered cock into her mouth. She sucked and licked the cum. I fucked inside her mouth to make it hard.

Soon we were ready for a second round.

*****_____*****

******_______******

Virgin predator

I stood naked in front of the mirror, checking my curves.

What made him love me? Or is it just lust? I wonder.

My breasts were still firm. They aren't too big but still had the shape and size to lure anyone.

No one would call me chubby; I am a medium sized lady.

My body hasn't lost its shape, just a little fat here and there.

I looked at my swollen cunt. My cunt lips were open. My clitoris stood aroused.

A smile twitched between my lips.

What should I do? Shall I go with him or not? That was my confusion. My mind said me to control my carnal urges but my body wasn't ready to listen.

What if anyone sees us together? Everyone will blame me. They will call me a bitch and a whore.

I am fifty one now. I am too old to be active in sex according to the society. Who are they to decide what a woman needs and stop her from having fun?

I was been single for almost seventeen years when my husband ran away with a girl never to come back. I was pregnant at that time and he needed a cunt badly.

In the shock, I lost my child and never had any physical pleasures until him…

I thought about him, his long hair, bright eyes and playful attitude and the care he gave me.

I am his teacher and he is my student. He is only twenty. He is young, energetic and explosively active.

What if anyone knew?

I was feeling worried.

As his teacher, I should not entertain this, my mind warned me.

But my body wanted more, can see my nipples harden and feel my cunt getting wet at the thought of him.

My sexual desires were rising. I wish he was here now.

The memories came to me, as clear as water.

Mahesh wasn't the brightest of students but was active in other curricular activities.

He wasn't a champion but he was good.

I liked him as a student though he was outspoken.

It was one day after the classes of the last day at college, I saw him sitting in the class alone.

I was ready to go home. I went in.

"Why are you here? Why are you not going home?" I asked.

The one week study leave was starting from tomorrow for the final exams.

"I knew you weren't left and you will come here." He stood up from his seat and walked towards me.

My purse was on the table.

"You should go home now and start preparing for the exams. It is way past college hours." I said.

He didn't reply. But I noticed he was looking at my body. His eyes were greedy. I felt disturbed. Or was his stare arousing something long hidden in me?

"Why are you staring at me like this?" I asked.

"You shouldn't come to college wearing sleeveless clothes."

His stare was at my chest.

"What is wrong with sleeveless dress? I am above fifty and no one would mind me wearing anything."

"That's what you think but for me you look like thirty five. I always lose control when I see your shaven, sweating underarms."

I was flattered to be honest.

"You look amazing and your sex appeal is glowing high."

"So you like only my underarms?" I asked. I can feel an unknown wave in my body. I liked the way he is speaking now.

He was standing right in front of me.

"I can see only underarms now. If I see other parts then I will say what all I like." He replied. Suddenly he lifted my hand and kissed under the arm.

I was stunned.

My body twitched for an instant.

I took a step back.

He took another step forward and again kissed and licked my underarms.

I was melting. His hot breaths hit my flesh.

It was a feeling I long thrived for but not now. No, I cannot encourage this. He is only a student.

"What are you doing?" I pushed him away. But he wanted more.

I was in his hold. Unknowingly I lifted my arm and his face dug under it. He licked and kissed continuously.

First time in all these years I was feeling a man. I was not me anymore. I felt the beads on my chest stiffening and a strange throb ripening between my legs. A mysterious sensation long forgotten filled my body.

Something was touching my thighs. I knew what it is. It was patting against me inviting to be freed. He pressed it against my legs.

I gasped. My breath was irregular now.

He freed me and unzipped his trousers. He released his prisoner and I couldn't take my eyes off it.

How many years have passed since I have seen a cock?

It wasn't huge but definitely strong and attractive. It twitched in its position tempting me.

"Uff." A gasp of hot air escaped from my already heated up body.

He took my hand and made me hold his cock. It shook in my fist hardening even more. I hold it tight as wanted it in my fist for a long time.

"Did you like it?" his stare directed into my eyes.

"Yes." I was honest.

"Can we stay here longer?" he asked, kissing on my lips.

"Yes." I felt my panties moist with my cunt honey.

He grabbed my boobs and started pressing them. Ohh, I wanted that badly.

I was waiting for this moment.

He crushed my tits with wild excitement as I stroked his cock with same passion.

He removed my top.

"Here?" I asked.

He threw it to the table.

"Yes teacher."

"Call me Leela." I demanded as he was crushing my boobs over my pink lace bra.

He walked me to the front row of the class room as he threw his clothes somewhere. He climbed on top of a desk and stood naked in front of me. His cock twitched at me.

Then he climbed down to chair. I walked towards him.

I grabbed his throbbing pole.

"In your mouth, Leela." He said.

I was reluctant at first. I haven't had a cock in my mouth for a long time. Even my husband gave his cock only a few times.

"What happened? You never had it in your mouth?"

I couldn't say I forgot to suck dick.

"Open your mouth." He said.

I obeyed my predator.

Yes, I wanted to be his prey. My body was in full submission.

I walked closer to him and opened my mouth. He entered in my mouth and he held my head.

It rested on my tongue for a moment and then quivered.

I wanted to take back my head but his hold was tight.

"Suck it now. You will enjoy, I promise."

I sucked as he said. I was starting to like what I was doing. His cock throbbed in my mouth.

As I licked and sucked his pole was getting harder and I was getting addicted.

Is his cock a drug? I know it is. A highly addictive drug!

He pushed himself with the rhythm of my mouth.

He was trying to get it as deep as he can.

Then he climbed down and removed my bra. I don't know which corner he threw that too. We both didn't care.

He nibbled my exposed tits and its stiff beads.

My cunt was throbbing.

He bit my nipples hard which made me shriek.

"I love you Leela. I was crazy for you."

I didn't know what to say. Part of me said this is wrong. He is my student. He is too young. But the other part of me said to get fucked by him. My pussy wanted a cock badly. After such long years my cunt is wet now. How can I deny my thirst? I never knew I wanted this so desperately. I was itching for this.

He was nibbling on my beads. I smile at the thought that he likes my boobs very much.

With one hand he pulled my black leggings down and I helped him do that.

He threw the cloth to some pat. He wasn't even looking. His face was dug into my tits. His tongue was trailing all over my tits, licking and sucking my nipples.

I squealed as he bit my nipples. He loved doing that. I liked it too since He wasn't biting hard to hurt me. It was soft yet giving a sweet pain.

We were standing in the centre of the classroom. I was having only panties on my body. He was now completely naked.

His young throbbing cock was in my hands. I felt like I want it in my mouth.

I kneeled and took it in my mouth. He was happy when I did that.

I sucked his cock well. I licked his balls and took them in my mouth. He was feeling pleasure as he moaned and twitched his hips.

"Leela, I want to fuck you now." he said. It was like he was my husband or boyfriend. He had that authority in his voice.

I stood up looking into his eyes. He kissed my lips.

He slowly pulled my green panties down. "Aah." He produced a sound of excitement. I looked down. My panties were wet and I saw my slimy white honey sticking to my panties. He was excited to see that!

He took the panties closer to his face and smelled it.

I was wondering what he was doing. Then I realized this was his time. That was why he was so fired up.

"This smell is indescribable. I never knew a cunt has such an incredible aroma."

I was flattered when He said that.

He licked my panties once to savor my honey. I didn't know what my honey tastes like. I was ashamed to ask him.

Then he licked all of it from my panties like he went crazy. Then he quickly came between my legs and started licking my cunt.

"Uff."

I can't say how I was feeling. The sensation made me quiver for a moment like an electric shock.

My cunt lips were open. My clit was raised high. His tongue sucked all the honey from my dripping cunt.

Then he bit my clit hard.

"Oh fuck." I screamed.

He jumped up and covered my mouth.

"Lower your voice." He whispered in my ears.

"That hurt." I said.

"Sorry, I was excited." He apologized.

He made me turned around. His hands brushed my ass and went between his cheeks. He inserted a finger in ass.

I was wondering what all things he is doing. My husband only watched my ass. He never bothered to touch it. This boy is inserting a finger in my asshole. Definitely he has gone crazy. He inserted one more finger and slowly pushed in and out.

I was allowing him to do whatever he wants to. I have completely surrendered to him. He was teaching me new ways of excitement and pleasure.

I bent myself a little for him to play well in my ass. He was standing at my side and I cupped his balls. His one hand was on my breast and other in my ass. His fingers were quickly going in and out.

I tried to moan as softly as I can.

He took out his fingers from my ass and slapped my ass cheeks.

Then he put them in my cunt. I was wondering when he was going to fuck me.

I couldn't wait to have his cock inside my pussy. I want a ride badly.

"I am mad for your ass, Leela. I love you. You belong to me now and forever."

"I am yours Mahesh." I replied. What made me say that, I don't know? I was mad with lust.

While I said he rammed his cock inside my cunt.

"Uff." I gasped.

After a long time I was having a cock inside my cunt. It was almost dry for seventeen years and now Mahesh has made it flourish with honey. How can I not love him?

He rammed into me again and again. I was squirming with the force.

"Slowly Mahesh." I said.

But he wasn't listening. Instead he was pushing harder.

"I love your cunt Leela. I want to fuck you again and again."

I was dripping honey again and he was fucking me easily now.

"Leela I am coming." He shrieked. "I want to come in you."

I wanted to say no. but before that I felt his cream in me and his thrusts slowing down.

He took out his cock from my cunt.

Loads of cream and honey fell down to the classroom floor from my cunt.

We both were panting heavily. I looked at him with gratitude and satisfaction.

"I want it every day. Will you give me Leela?" He asked. "You are my first."

He is a virgin. I was surprised. He did like he was experienced. My virgin predator.

I didn't reply. Instead I hugged him pressing my boobs onto his chest.

It was getting late.

"Come tomorrow Leela." He said. I was picking up my clothes from different parts of the classroom. He took my panties and said. "I want this. I want to smell it all night."

I had to agree. I kissed his cock. I was the first to claim its virginity.

We went home. The whole week we met at this classroom and had sex.

The next two weeks were exams and we couldn't even enter the college premises.

On the last day he had an unusual request.

He wanted to go to Goa with me for a one week tour.

He wants to fuck me all day and night to cope with the loss of two weeks.

I accepted in an instant. But now…

I looked at the mirror again. Tomorrow is the day. He will come in the morning to pick me. I am sure he will fuck me before we leave.

My body tickled at the thought. My wet became wet.

I am desperately counting minutes. I want this night to end fast.

Mahesh, your Leela is waiting with legs wide open for my boy.

*****_____*****

******_______******

Intentions

My name is Akhila. I am a housewife. My husband is a businessman. He is successful and busy. He was on tour regularly.

He loved me very much but he wasn't much interested in physical intimacy.

He did it occasionally like a machine which never made me satisfied. I was just a hole for him to release his cream.

He gives me a peck which can't be called even a kiss. He hardly touches my breasts. He never kisses my cunt. He never even allows me to suck his cock.

He finished his work in less than three minutes and go to sleep.

I was so disappointed. I watched some videos and had to self satisfied myself.

It was one of those days; I was watching a porn video.

My fingers were inside my cunt going in and out with great speed.

I was all alone in the house. My legs were wide open, skirt over my body and a table fan directed towards my cunt.

I can feel the heat of my breaths and the sweet aroma of my wet cunt. I licked my fingers covered in my slimy honey.

I mouthed a banana and made its outer wet and inserted into my cunt. I pushed it deep and pulled back.

At that moment the calling bell went on. I cursed whoever came at the door and stood up.

It was a salesman with some cosmetics and books.

We seated at the porch. I thought I will spend some time looking at them.

He had a big bag. He was around 25. He looked tantalizing.

I picked up a perfume from his bag. I was about to ask the price when I noticed he was looking at my belly.

I was wearing a sari and my belly was clearly open. I quickly corrected my sari.

He looked down troubled. I felt like tempting him more. I wanted to see his nervousness when he sees more.

I bent even more to take out a book when the sari slipped off my shoulders.

He could see my breasts through the low neck blouse. Maybe even my cream colored bra too.

Unhurriedly I rose up and pulled back my sari. I saw his stare through the side of my eyes. A smile twinkled between my lips.

I saw a slight vibration between his legs and I was sure he has got his rod hardened.

The thought made me horny.

I saw sweat beads on his forehead.

"You want some water, right."

"Ye…yes madam." He stuttered.

"Come inside with your things. Let us sit under the air."

I brushed his hand while giving the glass of water and gave him a luscious smile. Before taking the glass back I leaned towards him and gave a kiss on his cheeks.

He wasn't expecting that. He looked at me surprised.

I locked the front door and slowly removed my sari. He stared at my exposed abdomen and the belly button.

I invited him with my hands.

Like an obedient slave he came towards me and kneeled in front of me. He dug his head into my belly and kissed my belly button.

He tongued inside the navel and licked all over my tummy.

Then he stood up and cupped my face in his hands and kissed on my lips.

He nibbled my lips and tongue as we enjoyed the steaming union of our lips.

Honestly he was doing everything that my husband never did.

His one hand was behind my head and the other was on my ass pressing them with excitement.

He unhooked my blouse and removed it from my body. He greedily looked at my bra covered tits.

His face was in between the tits in the next instant. I unbuckled my bra for him and he took it off too.

He looked at my bare breasts for a moment and started sucking the nipples like a baby.

He licked, sucked and nibbled with a sensual passion as when he took his head up I saw my tits were reddened.

He undressed in front of me. He was more than he looked. His muscled body was exquisite. He had a long cock which stood erect teasing me.

I couldn't take my eyes off the hard pole twitching itself with lust.

I couldn't wait. I kneeled in front of him and kissed its cute head. I licked the long pole from head to root and mouthed it.

He pushed the cock inside and it touched my throat. I sucked his cock as he pushed it inside with force hitting deep inside my throat.

We went to the bed. I lay on my back. He kissed me again after climbing on top of me.

He nibbled my tits with great enthusiasm.

He bit my nipples softly. My nipples were hard like his cock.

His hand untied my skirt and pulled it down.

He turned me over and started to kiss my ass. He opened my ass cheeks and licked my butt hole. He was biting the cheeks in between. I moaned with pleasure.

I was again on my back and he started licking my moist cunt.

Ahh, I never felt so good before. He was like an expert with his mouth and tongue. I felt my honey skimming down and he licked most of it.

He opened my legs wide and lay on top of me. He rammed his long pole inside my cunt.

I hugged him tight and closed my eyes.

He pushed his cock again and again with force. The way he moved gave me a conclusion that he was good. He must be probably married, I thought.

I was panting as I was almost nearing my climax. I clutched a pillow and scratched his back as I had the best orgasm in my life.

He continued fucking me till he was about to come. He took his cock out and ran into the bathroom to release his cream in the commode.

I lay naked on the bed till he came back and dressed up.

I went to the hall room and bought a lot of items. I didn't forget to get his number. He promised he will be visiting me regularly.

He kissed my pussy again before he left. I went to my bedroom and looked in to the mirror.

I was reddened. He did an amazing work on my body. I opened my cunt lips and saw the moisture of my honey.

I can't say how much satisfied I was.

I stood in front of the mirror for a long time before going to the bathroom for a long shower.

*****_____*****

******_______******

Sexual fever

My name is Anand. This is a story about my first experience. I want to share with you that how your boring fever days could also be exciting.

I was studying in technical college.

My house was in the centre of a huge plot. Our neighbours were Ayyappan and his wife, Swati and their three children.

Their eldest girl is Arya, 26 years of age. Marriage proposals were coming for her but there was a fault in her stars. Her link with Mars is at imperfection.

I never understood these things.

They said she should only get married to a person with same star defects.

Swati Aunty was so beautiful and her children got her features.

Our families were close. We used to play together from our young ages.

Arya mostly used to be at our home. She was so helpful to my mother. She always helped her in kitchen chores.

Even I and my sister thought our mother always gave preference to Arya than us.

It was my vacation period.

One day I became ill. I went to the doctor and got the prescriptions. Doctor advised me to take rest for a few days.

That was a Saturday. The next day we had a marriage to attend.

Fever was low but I felt dizziness and body pain. So I decided to stay back.

Everyone else left with food prepared and set on the table for me.

I slept for a little while.

That time Arya came in.

I was still under the blanket. She checked my forehead. "There is no fever now. Why didn't you go to attend the marriage?"

"I still feel dizzy. And I am feeling cold."

She sat beside me and checked her cell phone. She was doing something, browsing and checking facebook or whatsapp when I was shivering.

She saw me and asked. "What happened, Anand?"

She could see me shivering.

She lay beside me and I adjusted a little to give her space. She lifted the blanket a bit and came inside.

I was on my back and she was on her side facing me.

I didn't felt anything that time.

She kept her hand on my naked chest.

I was wearing only a cotton *lungi* wrapped around my waist. I wasn't wearing a shirt.

She laid closer to me. Her big breasts were brushing my arms.

I felt an electric vibration passing through my body for a split second.

My rod was arousing.

She moved closer. She wrapped her hand around me. Her head was so close to mine and I can feel her hot breaths on my cheek. Both her tits were over my arms and chest as half her body was leaning over me.

"My heat will help you relax. You won't shiver now." I noticed the change in her tone. She was having a mood change.

My rod was in its full form now. It stood straight pointing skywards lifting my *lungi* and the blanket. I wasn't wearing any briefs.

Unexpectedly, Arya kept her one leg over mine, her lower part of the thigh too close to my erect pole.

I felt my cock quivering.

"Don't you feel comfortable now?" she asked. She wasn't calm but regularly moved, as her breasts rubbed me and her body brushed me.

Her knee touched my pole for an instant.

I hummed in a positive way.

My heart was beating fast. She must have noticed that as her hand was on my chest.

"I will hug you tightly so you will feel more warmth." She said.

She tilted her body again as her hug tightened. Her knee was touching my rod.

Yes, she noticed that. She lifted her head and looked down.

I am sure she saw the tent created by my cock.

I have a nine inch cock which made a really noticeable tent between my legs. She was not going to miss that.

I knew her hand going down from my chest. I knew my cloth sliding away from my cock. Her leg was off from my leg. After some time it was back again on my chest and her leg slid over my *lungi* sliding it sideways. Her thighs ride over my cock pressing it to my body. Her thigh was naked as was my cock.

She slid the cloth away from my cock and pulled up her skirt till her waist.

I can feel her wet cunt brushing against my hip.

She gave a little peck on my cheek and asked whether I am better now.

I replied yes and asked her how she was feeling.

"I need more than a hug to feel well." She replied.

She rubbed my cock with her thigh.

I turned towards her and hugged her. My lips met hers. My chest was against her breasts. My cock was between her thighs.

I nibbled her lips as she sucked them. Her breasts were getting squeezed against my chest.

"Oh Anand." She moaned.

She was feeling desperate. She was ready for anything and everything.

She wanted my cock and I wanted her cunt.

I can feel her heat, her thirst, and her lusty desires. I wasn't going to deny her the pleasure she was craving for.

I sucked her upper lips and she did my lower lips. I removed the blanket from our top.

My *lungi* was open and my ass open. My cock was between her thighs as she pressed it with her inner thighs.

I saw her naked part of the ass as her skirt was raised maximum.

My hand ran over her ass and inserted my finger into her ass hole.

She was in ecstasy.

Our lubricants leaked and made us wet.

I made her lie on her back and freed my rod. She opened her legs and I saw her swollen cunt. I was seeing a cunt for the first time.

"Lick my cunt." She moaned.

Small shards of hair raised above her clit as she must have shaved days back.

Her cunt looked like a lotus flower.

I took my face close to her pussy.

I smelled the sweet aroma of her flower. I kissed her cunt lips.

She lifted her hips in excitement. I heard her soft gasps. I saw her squeezing her breasts. She licked her lower lips.

She was so aroused with lust.

I started to lick her clit. With my each lick her body was twitching. I felt her small vibrations at her hips.

My tongue trailed over her cunt lips making her twitch even more. She was wet. She was melting like ice. I was on fire.

I opened her lips and licked her pussy. She was getting wetter. Her cunt was dripping honey.

She hummed, moaned and groaned with pleasure.

I bit her clit softly. She lifted her hips with ecstasy.

I licked the entrance of heaven.

Well, I am not a poet but I did write a poem with my tongue in her cunt for around twenty minutes.

She was moaning continuously.

"I am coming." She said.

She pressed my head between her thighs. I nibbled her cunt lips as her honey came in my mouth.

I drank it whole not letting even a drop go out.

It was now her turn. She pulled me towards her and pushed me onto the bed.

She kissed my lips and her lips trailed down to my chest. She looked at my 9 inch hard pole with excitement.

She held it in her fist and started stroking. I saw her eyes beaming with disbelief.

She used both her hands to stroke it. She was enjoying having my rod in her hands. "I didn't know you had such a big cock." She looked at me.

She kissed the pole head and tongued around it. She opened her lips to give entry into her mouth. Then she took it deep into her throat.

"Oh fuck." I never felt such a delight before. All my veins were getting tight and suddenly it happened.

Warm cream jumped out of my rod and it was in her mouth.

She took in her mouth and showed the cream on her tongue. I watched as she swallowed my cum.

She didn't let it soften as her hands stroked my cock with all her strength.

She sat on my top in such a way the my cock rested on me between her pussy lips.

She rocked her hips as her cunt lips rubbed on my cock making it rock hard again.

She wanted it now.

She rocked over my cock head as it went inside. She leaned over me and pushed her body back to help the rod get inside her pink flower.

She pushed again and again lifting her ass as almost half the length of my rod was inside her cunt.

She was finding it difficult to ride on my rod because of its length. It was tight too.

She asked me to do for her instead. She freed the stiff pole from her cunt and lay on the bed with her legs wide apart.

I leaned over her pushing my rod inside her. She helped the pole head inside her pussy.

She gasped with pain.

"Go in softly." She said.

I pushed my body and pulled back with gentle strokes as the rod rocked and rolled inside her.

My rod was only going in half the length so the next time I rammed into her with full force.

She screamed aloud as the cock went three quarters inside with great intensity.

She squirmed with pain and pleasure as I rammed inside her continuously.

Her soft moans turned into high pitch groans and yet she encouraged me to hit hard.

She was nearing her orgasm as I was almost at my climax.

My cock has swollen inside her and her honey seeped and gave a smooth friction to my movements.

I used all my might as I felt my climax almost certain.

We both came together almost at the same time. My cream filled her entire cunt. When I removed my cock the cream poured out with her honey.

We both looked at it with satisfaction.

We were breathing heavily.

"Let's sleep now. When we wake up, you will be perfectly alright." She said, breathing frantically.

I kissed her lips one more time and nibbled her nipples.

We lay together in the bed naked.

Sleep slowly took care of our tired bodies.

*****_____*****

******_______******

My wife's sister

I am a married guy. I live in Delhi with my wife and two kids. Nowadays I found out that my wife is not interested in me. She seldom does sex with me.

She is not as passionate as before. She doesn't take my cock in her mouth or swallow my cum. She was earlier so wild in sex but she has cooled down a lot.

Something has changed in her.

I talked to my best friend about this and he promised me to find out the reason. He advised me to take a month's leave and stay at some other place.

I decided to go to my ancestral place. It's been years. My wife and children stayed back at Delhi as they could not miss their work and classes.

I stayed at my house for three days and then went to my wife's house.

There I saw her sister, Neelam.

She has grown to be a sexy lady. I confess my sexual desires rise up seeing her.

As their wish I decided to stay in their house for a week. I tried to get as close to Neelam.

Neelam was becoming my ultimate craving. I badly wanted to fuck her.

I saw a spark in her eyes when she looked at me. It was not a look a wife's sister. Does she also have the same craving as me? I think so.

One day when I came back after visiting a friend, Neelam was alone in the home. The others will only return in the evening, she said.

I was happy to spend some time with her. We talked a lot about her studies and her aspirations. I asked whether she has any boyfriend. She smiled but didn't give me an answer.

She was wearing a red churidar top with long slit till waist and white leggings. I could see the lining of her panties through the slit. Her panties were dark colored and was clearly visible through her leggings.

My veins were on fire.

I saw her cleavage through her low neck top. I am sure she noticed that.

"You didn't say anything about your boyfriend?" I pushed her to know more.

"I don't have." She said. But her face said otherwise.

"Have you kissed?" I moved closer to her.

"Did you have sex with him?"

I saw a hint of lust along with dread in her eyes.

In the next instant I grabbed her and engulfed in a tight hug.

She was in a state of shock.

She tried to free herself.

Her tits were squeezed against me and my hold became stronger. My hard pole was against her lower abdomen. I squashed her ass with one of my hands.

"You are my sister's husband. This is wrong." She said.

I wasn't in a mood to hear that. I was blinded by lust.

I kissed her neck as my hand was in between her as cheeks.

"Your sister is not interested in me. I think she has an affair." I whispered to her.

I turned her and groped her tits, my cock pressing against her ass.

She was so soft and untouched. I made her touch my cock and rub on it as it was hardened like iron.

She was melting, her reluctance was slowly disappearing.

I use both my hands to grip her breasts. She started to moan. I knew she was ready.

She was starting to enjoy.

I released her hold and made her turn around towards me.

I kissed her and nibbled her lips. Her hands wrapped around me. She has surrendered to her sexual urges.

I let her tongue enter in my mouth and I sucked it. She was a passionate kisser.

Both my hands were on her ass, pressing them at will.

I wanted her so badly and she also wanted me. She unzipped me and took my cock out and stroked it gently.

I took her in my arms and walked towards the bedroom. I dropped her on to the bed and removed all my clothes. She looked at my naked body.

Her eyes were wide open with excitement. Her stare was on my erect penis as it throbbed in front of her.

I removed her churidar top. She was wearing a black bra. I quickly removed her bra too to make her lovely tits free.

Ahh, what a sight!

Her pink nipples were tight. Her tits were firm.

I pressed them and felt the softness of her flesh. I felt her hard beads in my mouth as I sucked and nibbled her nipples.

I pulled off her leggings and saw a navy blue panties. She was now wearing only that panties.

I can feel the adrenaline rush looking at her. She lay on the bed like a marble statue.

I kissed on her cunt over her panties. I can sense the heat of her cunt.

Her pussy was a little swollen.

I told her to have my cock in her mouth. She was reluctant at first as this was her first time. But when I wiggled my cock in front of her eyes she took it in her mouth.

She kissed the tip first and then kept the head inside. Her lips pressed the head of my cock. I forced my cock into her mouth. She sucked my cock.

She was good for a first timer. She did well. More importantly she enjoyed my cock in her mouth.

She nibbled my balls and stroked my rod as I was feeling the best pleasure in sex.

After sometime she freed my cock from her mouth. I sucked her tits again. She pressed my head in between her breasts.

I got hold of her panties and removed it. Wow, she had such a beautiful cunt, neatly shaved and clean.

It was a little swollen.

I dug my head between her thighs. I smelled her sweet pussy and inhaled the aroma of her moist cunt. I tongued over her clit and took it in my mouth and nibbled.

She squirmed when I did that.

My tongue trailed over her slit. I opened her cunt lips and started licking. Then I chewed her cunt lips.

I couldn't wait to get inside her virgin cunt. I fingered for a few seconds before forcing my cock into it.

She twisted in the bed with pain and pleasure. I pressed my cock fully inside and started fucking her.

Her moans turned into groans and her screams increased as my speed of thrusts increased.

I fucked her again and again until I came all guns blazing inside her cunt.

She also came at the same time as her wet honey ran down from her cunt onto the bed.

I rested on her after the climax.

She wrapped her hands around me as her lips were busy kissing all over my face.

It was around 2 pm.

We went to have lunch. After lunch we had sex again.

In the night I sneaked into her room and we fucked again. Instead of a week I stayed for a month and every night we had sex.

*****_____*****

******_______******

I am a single man who just came back from Dubai. I was working there as a supervisor.

After my two period completed I came home for a two month leave.

I am a shy guy though I look smart.

My parents went for a week retreat and I had to go my room mates' houses to deliver the packages they gave me.

I started with nearby distances. Almost every package I delivered and there was only one left.

This one was a big package. It was for a friends' wife and his newborn child.

I went after having breakfast in a plan to be back at home before night. I had to travel so many kilometers and unfortunately there was an accident on my way.

It consumed a lot of my time.

It was a difficult task to fine their home as I lost the track at least three times.

I could only reach there at dusk.

I met my friend's mother and his wife, Mansi. To my surprise she was my old school friend. I had a little crush on her.

Well, all the boys had crush on her. She was a damsel.

My friend's mother was too old and sickly. I should say Mansi had a tough job to maintain the house, looking after her old mother in law and now her six month old child and all the household chores.

She left her job to be a full time homemaker after three months of marriage.

Her mother I law wasn't in a good condition and they requested me to stay there at night just in case if they had any emergency at night.

I had no choice. Besides I can secretly watch my old crush.

We talked a lot about our school days. It seemed she was so happy to see me. She was getting bored at home.

We had dinner together. I helped her in her kitchen works as we chatted continuously.

At night the issue was where will I sleep? There were only two rooms. One was used by the old lady. That room had a foul smell. The second was using by Mansi.

Finally we decided that I will sleep in Mansi's room. She will sleep on the bed with her child and I will sleep on the floor.

Her room had an amazing fragrance of lily. She always wore lily based perfumes at school.

What was I feeling? First time in my life I was feeling comfortable around Mansi.

At the same time there was a wave of nervousness in my heart.

She told me to sleep on the bed as I am the guest. And besides that would be better for her to look after the child.

I lay on the bed. She at the edge facing away to breast feed her child.

I looked at her back. Her long jet black cover was open and spread across her back.

I wished to kiss her.

After breast feeding, she laid her child on the mattress on the floor.

She looked at me and asked. "Hari, you slept?"

I closed my eyes before she finished feeding. I didn't reply.

I heard the bathroom door opening and closing after a few minutes and then the sound of water falling down.

She is bathing!

She is naked, uff. The thought sent chills down my spine.

The sound of water stopped after a while. I opened my one eye a little and looked at the bathroom door and waited.

The door was opened and she came out.

She was only in a bath towel wrapped around her. Top half of her breasts could be seen. The towel was too short. If I had slept on the floor I could have seen her cunt lips. I felt my veins heating up. All the heat went to one particular position, between my legs. My cock was hardening.

I wished for something and ohh fuck, it happened. She dropped the towel onto the floor. She stood naked with her back facing me. Ohh, what a butt she has. My cock was harder.

Turn around, I whispered in my mind. I wish to see her cunt. I am sure it will be as beautiful as she is. Will she be shaved or hairy?

It didn't matter though. Seeing a pussy in real life was a big deal for me.

I was feeling desperate.

She pulled up a knee length cotton pants with floral design. She wore a grey top which had a full length zipper in the front.

I was sleeping at the far end of the bed and surprisingly she slept at the other end looking down at the toddler.

Her lily fragrance hit my nose hard.

I moved closer to her as if turned in the sleep. My hand rested too close to her body. She twitched a little and her ass brushed my hand.

She turned and lay on her back with one of her ass on my palm.

Ohh, it was so soft.

I wished I could squeeze them.

She turned towards me freeing my palm.

"Hari are you really sleeping?" she asked.

I didn't reply.

Next instant she grabbed my cock and pressed tightly.

"Uff." I jumped up.

"What the…"

"Fuck me." she said in a sultry voice. She pulled the zip down. Both her breasts were visible to me now. She removed the top. My cock was throbbing inside my trousers.

Since pregnancy she didn't had sex. Her husband went to Dubai when she was two months pregnant.

I was confident now. "Will you suck my cock?" I asked.

"Show me."

She doesn't need to say again. I stripped all my clothes and lay naked on the bed. My rod was towering skywards.

She was desperate and hungry.

She mouthed my cock and started sucking like crazy.

Just within two minutes I came. My cream was all over her mouth.

Well, we both were disappointed.

"I never took my husband's cum in my mouth. Yours is the first."

"I am sorry. It wasn't intentional. I couldn't control." I apologized.

"You are a virgin, aren't you?"

I shook my head.

She went to the bathroom to wash her mouth and came as I went to clean my cock.

"I will teach you." she said.

We kissed.

My lips trailed over her face kissing her eye lashes, her forehead, her long nose, her chubby cheeks and her lips.

Our tongues intertwined in a sensual union.

I wanted this night to be remembered.

I softly squeezed her tits and drops of milk oozed out.

Suddenly the child started to cry. She took the child and started to feed. I looked at her child sucking her breast. I sucked the other and drank some milk.

Then I started kissing her legs. I sucked her toe and licked her feet.

My tongue gradually came up licking her thighs. She asked me to slow down as she was feeding the child.

I wanted to see her cunt. I was desperate for the most beautiful sight.

I made her stand and removed her pants. She had hair all grown but the sight made me hard again. It shook as she looked at my cock.

She shifted her kid to the other breast as I kneeled down to kiss her cunt. She kept her legs wide. I saw her beautiful cunt lips. I sucked and nibbled her pussy lips as she moaned.

I fingered her as a sensual excitement filled me. I rubbed her clit with my thumb.

I looked again at her cunt. Her hair was curly and her lips were deep pink. The whole sensual area was a little swollen.

I smelled and the lily aroma mixed with her wet cunt scent pervaded my nostrils.

Then I kissed her ass when she walked away. She went to lay her kid on the bed and secured with pillow on both sides.

She lay on the bed with her legs open.

I nibbled her breast and poured the milk on her pussy with my mouth. I licked the cunt with so much love and she moaned continuously.

I poured some milk again on her cunt and some on my cock and entered her.

I rammed inside her with all my might. What a pleasure? I was fucking a girl for the first time. I never knew fucking gave so much delight.

I was riding her cunt with ease. My hips moved with rhythm. I squeezed more milk out of her tits.

"Fuck me hard, Hari." Mansi moaned.

My thrusts became faster and soon I came inside her. I stroked as I let all of my cum fill inside her cunt. My hot cream was in her lake. I kissed her lips and said. "I love you. I always loved you since school."

"I liked you too." She replied.

"I wished you would propose me."

I was stunned to hear that.

We fucked again at 3 am when the child woke up again.

In the next two months I visited them many times, stayed at their house and fucked Mansi number of times.

Our relationship was growing.

*****____*****

******______******

The girl next door

My name is Neeraj.

This is a true story of my first sex experience. It happened years back when I was twenty.

I hail from a remote village. My father was a wealthy man. I had the privileges of being born in a wealthy family.

My father was always on tour as he had a business especially exports. I see him hardly two or three days in a month.

My next door girl, Sruthi was a year elder to me. We were friends since childhood.

Her mom was a tailor and her father worked in our paddy fields.

She was always in our house doing household works. We already had an old lady who worked in the kitchen. Sruthi used to help her in her free time. But mostly she came to watch TV.

At that time TV was a luxury and that luxury only had in my house.

Sruthi got married two years back with a guy in our next village.

She has come now for the harvest festival.

I didn't have any experience in sex that time. My only knowledge came from a few books lend from some of my college friends.

When we grew up I had a soft corner for her. I don't know whether it was love. Maybe she was my first crush.

I really felt bad when she was married off. After her marriage only I realized that I missed her so much.

When she came to the village, she visited my house. She has become chubbier, I noticed. Her tits became big. Her body had more curves, her butt jumped out. She was a real sex bomb now.

She came to my room to inform that she is back in the village.

She was wearing a sari. I saw her belly and the curves on the sides. Her blouse was too tight for her boobs and I thought its hooks will break and her tits will be exposed.

She must have noticed my stare. She gave a luscious smile and walked away. I saw the ripples produced on her butt while she walked. I felt pressure between my legs and I saw my rod was hard.

Damn, she is hot.

That evening, my mom went to her mother's place.

"I will be coming back in the morning only. I will tell Sruthi to serve dinner tonight."

I nod absentmindedly.

None of our servants stayed at night. They all go to their respective homes.

After my mom left, Sruthi came home.

She wore a short knee length skirt and a loose top. As she walked her tits bounced inside her top.

There was no one else in the house, just the two of us.

She sat on the chair and started watching TV. I was sitting next to her on the couch.

She lifted her leg and kept the feet on the seat. Her skirt was forced down revealing her thigh.

I am sure she didn't do that on purpose. But I lost my concentration on the program running in the TV.

I was heated up by the sight of her thighs. My cock was hard inside my shorts. It twitched and I kept my hand over the shorts.

I crossed my legs so that she won't see the tent in between my legs. I tried to concentrate on TV but the scene was a steaming bedroom love between the hero and the heroine.

Oh fuck, I was losing all my control.

I wanted to touch her things.

I wanted to kiss her thighs.

She was this close to me. She looked at the bedroom scene in TV. I saw her biting her lips.

I raised my hands and purposely polished her thighs and scratched my hair. She didn't respond. She was all absorbed in the scene.

I put my hands down and kept on her knee cap. Still she didn't move or she pushed my hand away.

There was a steamy lip lock in the movie. I heard her gasping.

I twirled and nibbled very softly on her knees. She seemed unaware.

Seeing her unresponsive stance, I felt bold enough to trail my fingers down her thighs. My fingers were now in the inner side of her thighs gradually moving downwards targeting her precious private sector.

She moaned in a very low voice. Was it the scene in the movie or my fingers, I didn't know. My fingers were almost reaching her cunt; she turned her head and looked at me.

My hand braked there. I was in no position to take my hands off or keep it there.

I couldn't read what was on her face, what emotion she wore, but it wasn't pleasant.

I felt her heat, I saw her breasts raising up and going down fast. I can feel my heart also pumping fast.

What to do, I thought. Should I take off my hand or keep it there as long as she won't say anything or I proceed further.

My throat was dry. It was my first time.

Finally I decided to proceed. I will apologize later. I was desperate to touch her cunt. I was so fucking desperate.

My hand slid down too slowly like a snail.

Her eyes were affixed on me.

I touched her cunt lips. She was wearing nothing inside! No panties!

My little finger touched her slit. I felt her wetness, a slimy feeling that spread goose flesh all over my body.

"Are you going to fuck me?"

Was that a request or a question, I didn't know.

I didn't reply. Instead I took my hands off and leaned towards her. I kissed her on her lips.

When I returned to my original position she asked me to kiss again, this time more passionate and wild like the lip lock we just saw in the movie.

I couldn't deny her.

Our licks were joined in a hot union, we sucked each other's lips, and we opened our mouths and let our tongues twirl together. Our breaths were becoming heavy.

Sruthi held my head closer to her as she never wanted the kiss to end.

I cupped her big tits and started playing with the twin spheres.

She doesn't have a bra either!

She knew this would happen when I stared at her tits while she came to my room to inform that she was back in the village.

I was more aroused at the thought. I squeezed her tits harder. She moaned aloud and I knew it pained her a bit. Our lips were free for a moment.

I pulled her towards me. She alighted from the chair and fell on my body on the couch. Her big breasts squashed against my chest. My cock throbbed under her thigh. She held my face tight and against started to kiss and chew my lips. She was wild now. She greedily sucked my lips and tongue. Her steamy breaths were all over my face. She panted like a wild dog.

She is mine now. My Sruthi.

I am going to fuck her.

My hands ran over her back, down on her ass, caressing and squeezing at will. I lifted her skirt and moved my fingers between her butt cheeks rubbing her ass hole with high torque. She pressed me down with her big tits into the touch.

Her weight was pulling me down into the softness of the couch. She was all fired up with wild passion. Her rapid breaths exhaled hot air. She didn't give a rest to my mouth and lips.

She was so hungry and thirsty for sex. Or was it for me?

For a split second when our lips were parted I said. "I want to see you, complete."

She lifted off from me and quickly threw away her clothes.

"See me Neeraj." Her voice twitched with lust. I looked at her with desire. She parted her legs to let me see her cunt.

Fuck, I never had seen a cunt before.

She cupped her breasts in front of me and rubbed her clit. She put her finger through her slit and moved it inwards and outwards. She did it to teach me. I now knew what to do. I knew a little from the books I read.

I went towards her and kissed her tits. I nibbled her nipples and circled around them.

Her nipples were hard and aroused.

My mouth trailed down her body through her curves. I licked her belly button and kissed down till I reached her clit.

I kissed and sucked her clit and then tongued her slit. She moaned continuously encouraging me to go deeper.

She was wet now. I licked her cunt honey. She forced her cunt into my mouth. She was panting. The pleasure was taking over her.

I slowly raised and kissed her again and made her taste her cunt honey from my tongue.

She grasped my cock and stroked it. She started slowly but soon she did fast. She was so uncontrollable now.

I removed my clothes.

She pushed me onto the couch and climbed on top of me.

"I want your cock Neeraj. I badly want it."

She helped my cock into her wet cunt and stroked her ass up and down in rhythm.

She moaned and groaned aloud.

Nothing mattered to her now other than my cock.

Her strokes were faster now. Her ass thudded harshly on my groin.

I grabbed her tits and squeezed as hard as I could.

She wasn't stopping until I come.

I was worried what if I make her pregnant.

But I was unvoiced. I didn't want her to stop. The pleasure was mounting. Her wild moans filled the house.

I never knew a girl would be so wild while having sex.

I squeezed her tits harder as I was nearing the climax. My face twitched while the cream spurted out of my cock and filled her cunt.

Her strokes were now slow, her breaths were shallow now and I poured out my last drop inside her.

She continued for some more time until she had an orgasm. Her cunt honey watering between my legs and around my balls.

Tired, she leaned above me. Her lips gently kissed my cheeks and lips. She whispered. "I love you Neeraj."

How long we stayed that way we didn't know. But when conscience struck us, we jumped up. She has to go now.

But we didn't want to part. We wanted more.

"I will ask your parents to let you stay here all night. They won't reject my request."

I know she also wanted that.

We went to the bathroom and cleaned ourselves. We dressed up and walked towards her house hand in hand as lovers.

I asked her parents' permission to allow her stay at my house. I saw they were reluctant but they couldn't say no to me.

We walked back to my house, our hearts thumping with joy.

"I will fuck you all night." I whispered in her ears.

*****_____*****

******_______******

Carnal desires

She is my best friend in office.

We used to travel together to the clients and convince them. These travels got us close.

I knew the pattern lock of her cell phone as she knew mine. She used to check my Whatsapp messages and download and watch porn secretly from some Whatsapp groups.

She was active in social media.

One day I found out that she was in love with some guy while scrolling through her text messages.

She never told me about him.

When I asked about this she gave me the details. She said she was deeply in love with and will only marry him. She was a Hindu and he was a Muslim. I knew her parents will never accept this relation.

Well, the future is what we never know.

Their relation started through facebook and blossomed through text messages. They have seen each other through facebook photos but haven't met in real life. They were planning for a meeting soon.

She admitted she liked me a lot and if she hasn't met him she would have loved me.

Those words hurt me. I asked god why I didn't meet her before him.

One day she came to me with an unusual request.

Mridula and the boy, Salam had planned to meet at some place and she wanted me to go with her. The place was far away, more than three hours travel by bus and she was unsure of going there alone.

She has never travelled such long distances alone. And she felt some insecurity in meeting him alone.

On a Sunday we went to the bus station. We bought mango juice and some chips along with some dates before entering the bus.

We sat together. She tugged her hands around my hand and made it rest over her firm breast.

I felt heat between my legs.

Did she do on purpose, I didn't know.

She wasn't thinking of that. She leaned over me and was talking about a lot of things. We shared the chips and mango juice. She was enjoying my jokes and smiled wholeheartedly.

We looked a couple. A happy couple.

She was playful.

Three hours went like three minutes. I felt the journey ended even before it started.

Before alighting from the bus she asked to be at a safe distance away. She didn't want her boyfriend to see me.

He may think that she has two boyfriends.

I agreed, sadly.

She walked ahead of me. I carried the carriage bag with chips and juice. I hurried my way to the farthest corner of the bus station where I could get a clear view of her.

I saw the guy. He was handsome. His features were good and definitely he scored over me.

I saw her smiling with his chatter.

I thought he was cracking better jokes than me.

Yes, I was feeling jealous. I felt the urge to smoke. Though it was prohibited to smoke in public places, I bought a cigarette and blew out my frustration hiding behind a bus.

I could see her well. I saw her eyes searching for me.

I stood there for more than 90 minutes. I smoked five cigarettes in that time.

I am not a regular smoker you know. I am an occasional smoker. I only smoke after I have two or three pegs.

After those fucking 90 minutes I got a text saying that she is going with Salam to his house to meet his parents. She asked me to go home as Salam will give her a ride back home.

Fuck Salam, I thought.

Was I sad or angry or lost? I had no idea. I smoke two more cigarettes in succession as I saw her going with him.

At that moment a hand patted on my shoulder from behind.

Fuck, police!

My cigarette was burned more than half and I had to throw it away. I had to pay the fine for smoking at a public place. I know that fine will go to his pocket but a fine is a fine and I must pay it.

After paying the fine I walked towards the next bus to my home. I boarded the bus and I got another text. I thought to ignore it at first but how can I do that.

It said that Salam's friend was involved in an accident and he has dropped her at the bus station. She wanted to know whether I left already.

My heart jumped with joy.

I ran out of the bus and placed a call into her cell. I asked her where she was standing and walked towards her.

But the thought of Salam was haunting my mind and I was unable to show a happy face to her.

She understood that in an instant.

She asked to take her to the nearby beach. She was trying to cheer me up.

On the way we entered two or three temples and prayed together.

Well, I didn't, but I was silent. I don't know what she asked for herself from the gods.

As we walked she was leaning onto me. Her breasts were brushing my arms repeatedly.

I wondered why she didn't notice that.

She was someone else's girl but when she was with it felt like she was my girl. She behaved like I am almost her boyfriend. Almost!

We were at the beach now. We walked to the far end of the beach which was occupied mostly by couples.

Her words and behavior and her closeness to me was touching my heart. It was like she forgot about Salam.

I was changing. My mood was changing.

She jumped on my back wrapping her hands around my neck and asked me to carry her to the sea.

Her tits were squeezed against my back. I was feeling aroused.

I took her to sea. She loosened her hold as her breasts brushed my entire back while she landed on her feet.

She ran a few steps into the sea.

I stared at her like I was seeing her for the first time.

She turned towards me and splashed some salt water across my face. I ran towards her and she ran ahead. I grabbed her waist and picked her up.

I was feeling nervous to be honest.

I wasn't prepared for this day, especially after her meeting with Salam.

I didn't want to release the hold but I had to.

She was enjoying the time with me.

We saw the other couples kissing and hugging and doing other things.

She looked at me and asked do I need also something like that.

I looked at her eyes and saw her carnal desires provoking me.

I asked, are you comfortable with that.

She replied I don't mind having some fun with you. What's wrong in hugging and kissing you?

She walked towards a rock and pulled me towards her.

She slowly reached my lips and gave a gentle kiss.

I wrapped my hands around her. She was suddenly all fired up.

Her kiss became passionate and wild as she nibbled my lips, bit gently and sucked my tongue.

She was desperate.

I felt her body thirsty for more.

We forgot about Salam. Our lips united with ardor. Our tongues intertwined in our mouths. Our saliva mixed and our bodies quivered.

Her hugs became tight and she squashed her breasts against my chest. Our hips were joined together. We stood there like that for some time.

Then she released me with beaming eyes.

She saw a smile in my lips. Then she saw the bulge in front of my trousers.

She mocked me. "What is this? I was stabbing me."

I faked my anger and said. "That is a spear."

"I want to see the spear, Shiva."

"No."

"Please. I really want to see the spear."

In a moment I thought about Salam.

She asked again. "I really wish to see."

Fuck Salam. "See for yourself." I said.

She pushed me towards the rock and looked around to see anyone watching us.

She bent down and reached for the zip. She unzipped my trousers and took my hard rod out of my drawers.

She winked at me with a smile and caressed my rod and stroked it gently. It became rock hard inside her fist.

She kissed the tip and trailed around its head. My hands were between her long hairs watching her doing amazing things to my rod.

She took it into her mouth and stroked. I felt her tongue brushing my cock as she stroked continuously with her mouth.

Was I feeling love or lust or was it just my carnal desires taking over, I didn't know.

I loved what she was doing with my cock.

I knew if she continues doing like this I will erupt into her mouth. An unknown guilt was rising in my heart.

"Let's stop now." I said forcing her to free my cock.

"This is my spear now. You can close your eyes and pretend nothing is happening." She took the pole again in her mouth.

She took it deep as it touched her throat.

I was feeling all the pleasures of the world.

She took it out of her mouth and stroked my salivated rod with her fist. She licked my testicles, kissed them and nibbled them.

She was not her at that time. Her carnal urges were driving her crazy.

Sometimes my rod was in her hands and then in her mouth.

I couldn't do anything. I wanted more. I didn't want her to stop.

I held her head and pushed along with her tempo.

I moaned and groaned as I was nearing climax.

I knew my cream coming.

At the same time she increased her speed. My cock was in her mouth. I couldn't take it out in time. I came in her mouth.

She didn't spit. Instead she kept it in her mouth as I drained all my cream.

She licked my cock as he was going back to its usual form, soft and cold.

I saw her perspiring in the heat. It was 3 in the afternoon. She worked hard to get me into climax.

At that moment I concluded she was the one downloading porn from my Whatsapp groups.

"You have a lot of cream in you, Shiva. I want it again and again." She said, snickering at me.

I wondered what to say.

"Let's go now." she said.

We had to travel three hours to reach home.

She slept on my shoulders holding my hands to her breast.

She called me at night and we talked a lot about the day and my cock. She said she want to suck it again and again.

She said she liked me a lot and that was the reason she did what she did and she will always do it for me. When I asked about Salam she disconnected the call. I called her again but she switched it off.

After that day we used to hug and kiss before and after the office hours. It became a routine. She grabbed my cock whenever she got a chance.

We had no secrets between us. I saw her still messaging Salam. She was still in love with him. Am I just a passing fantasy?

She was an enigma to me. Or is she loving him but teasing me as I am her toy for lust?

I checked her messages again to see how her relation was going on with Salam. It was going strong. The guy seemed nice and decent.

One month later she invited me to her home for her sister's engagement.

The invitation was only for me. I knew she hasn't informed Salam also.

I went to her home. She asked me to come home directly. I was a bit late and my cell phone was ringing continuously with her calls.

When I reached her home she was alone. Everyone has already left.

She cribbed and complained of my irresponsibility but when I hugged her tight she became happy.

"Shiva, you were late purposely for only this."

She was wearing a red knee length top with long slit reaching even above her waist and pink leggings.

"How am I looking? Am I sexy?" she asked playfully.

She knew where my stare was at. I was looking the lining of her panties which was clearly visible above the skin tight leggings.

She lifted the back piece of the top high enough for me to see her ass. I saw the beauty of her through her tight dress.

"You like it, my ass. What do you think?"

To be honest, I lost my control. Fire burned in my veins and my cock throbbed inside my trousers. I couldn't take my eyes off the two amazing semi spheres of her back. Her butt was well shaped.

"Can I touch?" I asked; my throat was dry.

"You don't need my permission, do you?"

I grabbed them in an instant. I bent and kissed her ass over her garment.

"Don't you want to kiss m front too?" she asked lusciously.

Oh, she wanted that.

I can feel the heat of her pussy as I kissed her cunt repeatedly.

"We are getting late for the engagement." She reminded me.

We left her home instantly. She sat behind me on my motor bike hugging me tight. Her firm tits were pressed against my back. Her one arm wrapped around me and the other rested on my throbbing cock.

"I wish I could take your spear now in my mouth." Her voice was euphoric.

We arrived at the temple on time.

After the engagement she introduced me to her family. It was a low key affair. There were hardly hundred people attending the ceremony.

We had lunch together.

I had a feeling that she was introducing me as her boyfriend. Soon most of her relatives left. Her family and I were left.

I asked her permission to leave. She said she wanted a short ride with me before I leave.

We left the home and she showed her beautiful village to me.

Then it suddenly rained. We saw an old house nearby. I took my bike there. We ran to the porch of the house. It was abandoned.

Shrubs grew all around the house. There were trees with lot of branches. The sky was dark and the rain was getting heavy.

We were drenched in the rain. I saw the rain drops dripping from her head. Droplets were on her upper lips.

Suddenly she hugged me tight. Her warm breath hit my chest. I also wrapped my hands around her tightly.

Our carnal desires were rising.

My cock was throbbing as it was like an aching snake searching a hole to hide.

We were out of control now. She filled my face with her warm kisses. She breasts were rising fast as her breaths became quick.

She unbuttoned my shirt and kissed my chest and abdomen. Her tongue circled around my nipples.

My hands ran all over her back.

Her lips were on mine. She nibbled my lips and tongue. She bit my lower lips hard. I felt really bad pain and screamed.

"I want it now Shiva." she cried.

My cock was exerting pressure at her front.

I turned her around and my cock squashed between her butt cheeks. I kissed her ears and the back of her neck. My arms wrapped around her belly. I lifted her top a little and hand snaked its way through the slit on to her belly button. I circled my finger inside her belly button as she pushed her ass back to give more pressure onto my hard rod.

I unzipped her dress from behind.

She removed the top and I stared at her beautiful breasts hiding inside a white bra.

I grabbed them and started to squeeze them.

Her hands were searching between my legs. She got hold of my rod and she undid my trousers.

Her sultry gasps were heating up.

I removed her bra to free her half round wonders. They looked firm but were soft like soap bubbles. I kissed them, licked the nipples and sucked and nibbled like a fanatic. Her tits turned red after I lifted my face from them.

Mridula was stroking my cock with passion.

My trousers and briefs were half down. I quickly removed my unbuttoned shirt and half pulled trousers and under garment. I stood bare in front of her.

She pulled her leggings down and threw it away into some corner of the porch.

She looked lustier in her blue panties. She had an amazing body.

I pushed the front door of the house. We heard something clanging to the door. I pushed again with more force. The door opened. I saw the lock on the floor.

We went inside. She took a broom and seeped a corner of the room.

She threw the broom away and slept on the floor. She was ready to have sex. She wanted it badly. I wanted it badly.

Nothing else mattered, just me, her and our carnal desires.

I looked at her admiring the beauty of her well crafted figure. She wasn't too thin, but fleshy. Her curves were perfect. Her breasts were round and solid. Her hair spread across the floor. Her horny face was beaming with beauty. Her thighs looked like ivory tusks. The blue panties added a sensual splendor to her.

"I don't want to forget this day Shiva."

"You will never forget." I promised.

I was on top of her. My lips met hers.

I removed her panties and lowered my head between her thighs.

I kissed her slit and nibbled her clit.

"Aaaaahhhh." She screamed with lust.

I nibbled her clit continuously as she wriggled with pleasure. I opened the petals of her rose flower and my tongue trailed up and down her cunt.

She lifted her hips, her eyes were tightly closed and she squirmed and moaned.

"Shiva… I want your spear… it is mine… spear in my mouth…" She blabbered.

I turned 180 degrees and was on all four. My cock touched her face and she took it inside her mouth. I pushed it deep inside her mouth and I could feel the tip entering her throat. I rammed continuously into her head, slow but deep.

My head was between her thighs licking her cunt. A strong scent along with heat was coming from her cunt.

"Shiva, fuck me, I want it now." she moaned. It was hard for me to understand what she was saying as my cock was entering and exiting her mouth with easy movements.

I know I shouldn't waste my time.

She is my girl and I should claim her first.

I returned to my normal position and lay over her partially. I guided my cock into her wet cunt. She parted her legs wide. Her cunt was tight and I forced my rod. It was hard like iron. She wriggled with pain. She shrieked loud but was silenced by a thunder.

The rain was getting heavy outside the house.

I pushed again with greater force and my cock head was inside. She cupped her cunt and screamed.

I waited for a moment. "Don't stop I want the spear inside." She was panting.

I took a deep breath and pushed again. My cock was a quarter inside her cunt and I heard her scream aloud.

I squeezed her breasts and locked my lips with hers and I tried to insert my rod deeper into her tight and moist cunt.

I felt her squirming under my body. I retracted a bit as the cock had only its head now inside her cunt and rammed with full force.

Her body twitched and she but hardly on my lips making a cut. We both felt the taste of blood in our mouths.

I slowly pulled my hips back and pushed again. And again. And again.

She sucked my lips and the blood. I increased my speed and she groaned with each push. She cupped my butt cheeks.

"You wanted this spear, have it."

"Yes this is my spear." She was twisting with pain.

Now the movements were easy. I hit her insides continuously with more force and speed. She shrieked with each thrust.

I felt I was about to come and removed my cock in an instant. I came over her thighs.

She was panting heavily.

"Your spear is amazing Shiva." She was rubbing her clit. I inserted my fingers inside and pushed and pulled them rapidly. In a few minutes she squirted. Her honey spurted out as from a water jet.

"That was great fun." She said.

"The fun is about to start." I snickered. I can hear the thunder rumbling in the skies and the rain pelting down heavily. "I am going to do again. You want to remember this day forever, don't you?"

She looked at me with lust as she wiped my cream from her thighs and licked.

"Oh yes." She said. "Give me my spear."

She took it again in her mouth. My cream was still at the tip. She licked the head and trailed all over the cock body and nibbled my balls. She stroked my rod with her hands.

I kept her head still and pushed my rod into her mouth. By the time it was hard again. I kept pushing into her mouth.

When I tried to take it out she demanded she want my cream in her mouth. I pressed deep into her mouth and my cock was touching her throat.

I made her lie again and rammed again into her moist cunt. She moaned loudly. I was not going to stop. I was going in again and again and she cried out with both pain and pleasure.

She has surrendered to me as my cock was continuously exploring her honey soaking cunt.

I took my cock out as I was nearing climax. She nibbled my balls again before taking 'her spear' in her mouth.

I came in her mouth filling her mouth with my cream. She sucked even the last drop from my cock and swallowed.

I helped her rise on her feet and bent forward to lick her cunt. I opened her pussy lips and licked her cunt. I nibbled the clit and cunt lips as she was reaching towards ecstasy.

I inserted my fingers and shook them vigorously while she rubbed her clit. She came spilling her honey from her cunt. I licked her honey as she had orgasm.

We both smelled of cream and honey.

We walked out into the rain and washed ourselves. The whole area was vacant and we kissed in the rain.

We hugged in the rain and my hands were squeezing her ass cheeks.

"I want to do in the rain." I whispered in her ears.

"No," she said. "I am tired. My pussy is paining."

I could see the swell of her pussy.

"You asked for it. I can't stop now. The climate is driving me wild. And rain soaked Mridula standing in front of me naked is making me wilder."

She was indeed a wonderful sight.

I cupped her breasts and circled my fingers around her hard beads.

"Can I?" I asked her.

I know her cunt was burning but I really wanted to do again. I wanted her to remember every moment of this day. I wanted her to forget Salam.

She sighed. She didn't want. I thought she would deny. But she surprised me.

"Do it. You are the boss today." She took my cock in her hands and stroked it.

She was ready!

I lifted one of her leg and wrapped around her with the other hand. She helped my cock to enter her cunt.

I did again. I fucked her hard in that heavily pelting rain.

We both had our orgasms together. She rested her head on my chest. Our privates were really burning. The throb was exquisite. My cream was in her cunt and her honey soaked my rod.

I didn't take it out in time and she was also tired to say so. We stayed in the rain in the same position for a long time and then I asked.

"Don't you want this spear every day?"

She looked into my eyes. I saw a spark so unexplainable tingling in her eyes.

She hugged me tight as she was unable to face me. I wrapped my arms around her.

I heard her saying. "I love you Shiva. I want you."

That's what I wanted to hear. I know how to throw the thorn out. Salam will be fucked.

Mridula is my girl. I decided.

$$$

Can you believe that tomorrow is our wedding day?

Yes she is my bride.

*****_____*****

******_______******

My hot neighbor

We were ready to go to the airport. My neighbor Augustan was going to Dubai.

He got a job as a manager in a production company. It was a dream job for him.

He had sent hundreds of applications all around the globe before he got his job.

He badly wanted to go to Dubai. All his childhood friends were working there.

He was so happy and yet there was a hit of disappointment in his face. He has to leave his wife here as his visa sanctioned was not a family visa.

Augustan is twenty eight and his wife Nina is twenty five. They were married for five years. But they were not fortunate enough to have a baby yet.

Augustan recently bought the house in our neighborhood. He was living in his ancestral home before.

Both our families became close in the early days itself. I am twenty one, studying for final year Arts in college.

Nina was an amazing beauty. She was slim and tall, even few millimeters taller than Augustan. She is one or two inches taller to me.

She had a perfectly shaped body. She had green eyes, long nose, red lips. Her neck was a precisely crafted work of a genius.

She mostly wore red dresses which made her fair skin glow more.

She was the subject of chats between my friends. They were all jealous to see me freely interacting with her.

I became close friends with Nina. I had enough freedom to put my arms around her shoulders and walk closer to her gripping our bodies together.

My friends asked me to introduce them to her but I was reluctant. I knew what they wanted. They wanted to fuck her. Their hearts were filled with lust.

I wasn't going to let that happen. She is my favorite friend.

Though it was only friendship between us, I felt much more. My carnal desires were arising inside me. I felt my body awake with desires.

I didn't know what she was thinking about me. I didn't know how to approach her.

After Augustan left, I became more than a visitor in her house. I became a member of the family.

Augustan's old mother came to stay with her as she couldn't stay alone in the house.

I was always busy, buying groceries for her, assist her in shopping and go to banks and even routine checkups in hospitals.

Augustan's mother used to drink liquor at night. She takes two neat pegs of whiskey before having dinner. Sometimes she offered me a peg or two secretly. In those days I slept at Nina's guest room so that my parents wouldn't know that I have had liquor.

Two months passed. My desire for Nina was growing day by day.

One evening, I was pouring liquor to Augustan's mother. Nina was standing near me. She had a shot and offered me to have one.

Augustan's mother was happy and she drank more than her usual quota of two.

We had to carry her to her bed. When we were putting her to bed I hugged Nina. She didn't resist me.

Her mother in law was almost asleep in the bed.

My carnal desires were paramount. I was behind Nina and my arms around her belly.

My rod was awake and was pressing behind her.

How long we stood like that, I didn't know. But I felt her breaths became irregular and her lusty gasps steaming out.

My rod muscle was fully hard and tightly pressed to her ass and she pushed her ass back to keep the pressure intact.

"Let's go to my room." she whispered. I can see her breasts rising and lowing with each breath she took.

I freed her and we walked into her bedroom. She secured the door.

She was all horny and ready to explode.

She was wearing a sleeveless red satin silk nightwear.

We hugged again. I pressed her tits and ass at will. Her hands ran all over my body.

This was my lucky day. I have Nina with me ready to do anything. She is horny for my cock. Her round tits and butt are under attack by my hands. Soon I can see her all naked.

Uff, goose bumps filled my flesh.

Then she grabbed my cock. It was ready to burst out.

She pulled my trousers down and looked at the tent on my underwear. She smiled.

She pulled it down too and held my cock in her fist and stroked it. She did it very fast. I lost all my control. I wanted to do a lot of things, but...

Fuck...

That was a failure.

I came in a minute. My cream was on her nightwear and hands.

I really felt ashamed. I pulled my clothes up and unlocked the door. I silently went out of her house. I didn't even say a good night.

I felt very bad. I couldn't even get my cock inside her cunt.

I didn't know how I am going to face her again. I was proud of long cock. I had the best cock among my friends.

And yet...

I failed her.

I felt like a loser.

I tried to avoid her the next whole day. I didn't even go there next two days.

But then one day Nina called for me. She wanted to buy something and I should take her in the bike.

I was worried what would have she thought of me about the fast ejection.

I had no other option but to face her. After the college I went there. Nina saw mw and went inside.

I talked to her mother in law. She complained that I ignored them and asked why I didn't visited them last few days.

I said I wasn't feeling very well.

She gave me some money. "My bottle is finished. If you are going out buy a liter for me."

Nina came to us; she was ready to go some purchase. She was wearing jeans and red t-shirt.

When we reached an abandoned area, she asked me to stop.

She hugged me from behind, pressing her tits against my back.

"That was your first time, I guess."

"Yes." I said, shyly.

"I need to buy some pills for protection. You must come today."

I couldn't believe her words. She didn't mind what happened with me that day.

"Relax your mind when you come. You can't enjoy a good fuck when your mind is disturbed."

She was stroking my cock. It was already aroused.

"You also have two pegs with mummy. That will help you." she whispered in my ears. Her stroking became strong. "I want to see it now."

I got off the bike and lowered my jeans and drawers. She came behind and stroked my cock until I came. This time I took few more minutes than the other day to explode.

Though it was still fast, I was feeling confident.

"Come on let's go." she said.

As she said I had two rounds of liquor and we made the old lady drink more. We carried her to the bed and were off to sleep soon.

Then we went to Nina's bedroom.

My heart was thumping fast. She was wearing the same red satin silk night wear she wore the other day.

I saw her hard nipples popping out of the night wear. She wasn't wearing any bra. I wondered whether she had panties too.

That amazing sight was enough for me for arousal.

I hugged her from the front and her boobs were against my chest. My hands trailed her back and went down to her butt.

She wasn't wearing panties too. She was all prepared tonight.

She understood my tension. She said. "Easy stallion, easy."

She unbuttoned my shirt and removed it. She licked my chest and nipples. Her tongue trailed down to my belly button.

I was experiencing the pleasure for a female seduction. She stripped my remaining clothes off.

My rod was standing erect and ready for action.

Nina gently caressed my cock and kissed its head. She licked the tip as her fingers nibbled my testicles. She took my whole rod into her mouth and fondled with passion. It went deep into her throat.

Uff, I was feeling the best pleasure in my life.

Was it the liquor, I don't know, but this time my cock didn't spit fire quickly. She was holding under the root of my cock tight to stop the flow. I felt my cream was stopped in its route to her mouth.

She was moaning as she ferried my hard muscle inside her mouth. Her speed increased and I produced sounds with ecstasy.

The moment she released her hold on my cock, it spit white fire. My rod was still in her mouth and I know the whole juice went inside her mouth.

I saw her swallow the whole cream and yet she was still fondling with it. My cock was getting soft but it seemed she didn't want to get it out of her mouth.

Once again I felt a little disappointed as I could insert my cock in her cunt.

I knew she also wanted that. She hasn't had a fuck for two months as Augustan has gone abroad. He will come back only after two years.

I was wondering what to do next.

She stood up and removed her night wear. I saw her, naked and aroused. Her dark beads were popped out. She was radiating heat of lust.

I could feel a spicy scent around her and I knew that was coming from her cunt.

Uff, what a sight!

That was the first time I was seeing a lady bare in front of me. Her tits were so beautiful and round. Her slim well curved features were driving me crazy. She has shaved her pubic hair. I knew in an instant that she shaved today after we came back from purchase.

I nibbled her round tits and licked all over her body. I kissed her like crazy on her tits, around nipples, belly, neck, chin, lips and behind her ears. My lips ran all over.

"Taste my cunt." She said.

She kept her legs wide open for me. I kneeled before her, my head was right against her spicy cunt, I got the strong heat emitting from her cunt.

Her cunt lips were pink and it was a sight to behold. My first encounter with a rosy cunt!

My whole body trembled with excitement.

"Kiss the clitoris first and lick on it. Slowly lick down to the slit. Aah." She moaned.

I did as I was told. I nibbled on her clit, trailed long enough to cover her entire cunt to her clit. She was wet and it tasted bitter sweet.

Her heat and aroma was biting into my nose.

I was experiencing a cunt for the first time but as she said later I did well for a first timer. I was weird and mad with my mouth and tongue.

I sucked one of the petals of her cunt and pulled gently with my lips.

"Aah." She gasped with lust and pleasure.

I felt her honey leaking into my mouth. I took it all. She wanted me to have her cunt honey.

She shook her ass with rhythm as the honey dripped into my mouth. She pushed my head closer to her cunt. I knew I should drink.

Tonight she was my sex teacher.

When she finished she released me and pulled me up. She went down and took my soft, sleeping cock in her mouth. She rubbed, licked, sucked and nibbled my cock and my balls.

I was hardening again.

She lay on the bed with her legs open.

Nina asked me to insert my rod and ram her.

She lifted her hips for me to enter her easily. She placed my cock at her entrance and asked me to push. Smoothly my cock went inside her wet cunt.

"Thrust hard; fuck me like you mean it."

I shook my body as I pushed harder and harder into her pussy. I felt a lot better now. I was growing in confidence.

I forced my cock deeper and deeper into her cunt as she rubbed her clit vigorously. My balls hit her perineal raphe repeatedly. I was focused on my cock getting deeper into her cunt. My body was supported with my hands stationed on both her sides.

My cock moved in and out of her cunt like a piston.

"I will come on top." She said.

We changed our positions. I lay on my back, my rod ready to shoot skywards.

She kissed my cock and nibbled my scrotum before sitting on top of me with my rod inside her.

Her hips danced over me, her butt hit over my pelvic area. Each time her ass hit me, I could hear the soft thud.

She leaned onto me and kissed me. I grabbed her tits and started crushing them hard with my hands.

"Aah." She screamed.

Her pace increased and I applied more pressure on her boobs.

She did like an expert; she slowed down in between and wriggled her ass then again did faster.

"Fuck me from behind." She said as she climbed down. She bent forward with legs wide supporting her body against the wall.

I tried to insert into her ass.

"Not in my ass, put it in my pussy."

I rammed inside her cunt again and fucked her harder. I was comfortable in this position and pushed harder and harder inside her cunt.

I kissed the nape of her neck and licked behind her ears.

I can feel my cock scratching against her cunt walls.

She was horny and wild and made sweet pleasurable moans. I felt the moisture of her cunt on my cock as I guided my rod in and out with greater force.

I was leaning over her, one hand wrapping around her abdomen and other cupping one of her breasts.

She pushed her ass synchronizing with my rhythm and my cock went deeper inside hitting her cervix.

She rubbed her clit well with her fingers and the other hand was on the wall for support.

She gasped, moaned and groaned make me more wild. I felt her other boob dangling with the tempo.

"Ohh, that's it…that's how you do…" she encouraged me.

I filled her insides with my cream. I slowly pushed to eject till the last drop and took my cock out.

She looked at me with satisfaction.

I know I did well. Her eyes were beaming.

"Sleep with me tonight, in my bed." she said.

I nod my head.

"Not just tonight but every night. I want a ride every day."

I promised her I will give her the ride to heaven every single night.

Next day at night as usual I went to her house. I was happier and more confident.

She was waiting for me. I was eager to make her mother in law drunk and drop her into her bed.

After some time there was some power failure. The entire village was under darkness.

We were sitting in the porch. Nina went inside to get the emergency lamp.

I was desperate for her presence all the time. I wanted to hug her before I could her mother in law to sleep.

I apologized to her and went inside with Nina.

The emergency lamp was inside Nina's room and she guided me there. My hand was in hers.

Inside the room she hugged me tight and kissed me like crazy. Her boobs were pressed against my chest.

I was heated up in an instant and I knew she was horny. My cock was erect and wants to explore her sweet cunt.

She was wearing a top and a skirt.

Our hot breaths were making the room warm.

My hands were moving behind her back, trailing down to her ass.

She was wearing nothing inside. I pressed her butt cheeks.

We couldn't stay like that for a long time.

We didn't want the old lady be suspicious about us.

She had the lamp in her hands. I walked behind her, my hand cupping her ass.

Nina compelled the old lady to have two more rounds as we both had a shot each.

Then I helped her to her bed while Nina guided us with the light. We headed to her bedroom to have our fun.

Even before entering the room I hugged her from behind. My cock was trying to find its way into her hole and gave a lot of pressure on her ass.

She bent her neck and I kissed her on her lips. My tongue snaked into her mouth as she opened for a little moan.

I pulled her top up and she dragged her skirt down. I stripped my clothes away with her.

She engulfed me in a warm hug as her lips were busy kissing my eyes, my forehead and lips.

She nibbled my lower lips as I did her upper. She patted my tongue with hers and together they twirled passionately.

My finger was between her butt cheeks trailing up and down with force.

My cock was quivering at her lower abdomen searching for an entrance.

She lowered her hand and got hold of my hard muscle and started stroking it.

I inserted my finger in her tight asshole.

Our lips were united in a steamy lock.

We stood there for a long time.

Then she kneeled before and took my rod in her mouth. She stroked it with her mouth with quick movements of her head.

She nibbled my balls and licked them and again took my stiff pole inside her mouth.

I knew she wanted my cream in her mouth.

I pushed my hips along with her. Her fingers wriggled my testicles.

I lost all my control and came in her mouth. She swallowed everything but she didn't take it out of her mouth. She was still stroking hard and fast.

I wanted a break and tried to free my pole.

"Let me do what I am doing, otherwise you won't be able to satisfy me enough. Slowly we will increase your timing."

I knew my cock was not mine anymore. She has the authority over the pole. I won't deny her. I already promised her I will fuck her and show her heaven every night.

My cock was getting stiff again.

She made me sit on a chair and sat over me. Her nipples were in my mouth. I licked all over her firm beads and nibbled them.

She guided my pole into her cunt. It was moist. Her hips danced with rhythm and her ass thud continuously on my thighs.

She was really on fire. Her moves were fast and with heavy force. She pressed my head between her tits. I found it hard to take breaths but she didn't released. She was coming.

Her cunt spilled honey all around my cock and it dripped down to my pelvis.

She stood up and leaned towards me. I licked her moist cunt and the warm honey drooling from it.

After licking her cunt clean I pushed her towards the bed and made her bent down supporting on the bed.

I went in from behind as that position was comfortable for me.

I rammed inside her with great force as my balls hut her ass. I grabbed her tits with both hands and entered again and again in her pussy.

I took a lot of time as I continuously rammed inside her cunt with all my mighty strength. She was moaning loud. My cock head went deep inside and hit her cervix.

My pushes became shorter but faster. We both were fired up.

I held her hips now to add more pressure to my forces. I was nearing climax. Her screams told me she was also having an orgasm.

We came together. Both our cream filled her cunt. As soon as I removed my pole from her cunt loads of our creams streamed out on to the floor.

We were panting heavily. We were all sweating in the heat.

At that moment electricity came.

We looked at each other. Sweat was running down between her tits. Tiny bubbles of water covered all over her body.

"Let's bath together before sleeping." Nina said.

That would be amazing. I thought.

We went to the bathroom and stood under the shower hugging each other.

Cold water ran down through our body and we felt the chill together. Goose bumps rise on our flesh.

She was stroking my soft meat continuously.

She wasn't done. I wondered.

Before we finished our bath my cock was hard again. It throbbed vigorously inside her fist.

She asked me to lick her cunt while she dried her upper body with the towel.

She used the towel to dry my hair while I was ardently licking her clit and cunt and nibbling her cunt lips.

She quickly wiped the water from our bodies and I again tongued at her rosy cunt. I nibbled at her cunt, trailed down to her perineal raphe and her ass hole. Her knees were bent and she was in a half sitting position exposing her asshole also.

I was under her enjoying the pleasure of licking her beautiful pink cunt lips and its inner parts as she opened the lips for me. She pressed my head towards her pussy and I forced my tongue inside her cunt.

Her body quivered as she came, all her honey directed in my mouth. I gulped it all.

She freed my head and went down on all fours inviting me to fuck her from behind in a doggy position.

I accepted her invitation gleefully and entered from behind. I cupped her cunt and leaned over her to kiss the nape of her neck. I lick the entire back of her neck and ride my tongue towards her ears.

All this time my cock was hitting the insides of her cunt grazing the walls of her pussy.

She was panting heavily and I was feeling tired but my pride wouldn't allow me to stop.

I had to fill her cunt again with my cream.

How long we did, how long I fucked, we had no idea. It felt like ages and my cock was paining, its outer skin aching when I came for the third time that night.

Nina licked my cream covered cock clean and then washed it with water. She splashed water into her pussy and cleaned the juices. She wiped both our genitals and we walked towards the bed.

When I checked the watch I realized with astonishment that we were indulged in action for more than three hours.

I hugged her tight and kissed her before saying goodnight.

We lay on the bed naked. My arms were wrapped around her. Nina was still holding my cock gently stroking.

Is she trying to wake it up again?

Will she make me fuck her again in the night?

*****_____*****

******______******

My name is Shivdas. But I am usually known as Unni. I am 26 years old.

I work in a footwear show room in accounts section. There were nine other people working here other than me, five people at the ground floor and four on the first floor.

Shreya is my accounts partner. She is 24 with normal height and with features matching her height. She is fair. She is married. She is hot. Her lips were blood red. Her breasts were little bigger than normal. She had a great ass. Her perfume was tantalizing.

It was given to her by her husband who works abroad. No kids and living with her in laws.

My cock always gets hard when I see her. But I tried to control my urges. I gently brush it above my trousers.

Why the fuck are you making me crazy? I usually ask in my mind.

We always sat next to each other at the cash counter and it was hard for me to control my rod. I used to jerk off in the bathroom thinking about her.

She became my desire. I badly wanted to fuck her. But I know that would never happen. I decided to approach when I get a chance.

One day she accidentally dropped her pen to the floor. It fell between my legs. I was busy typing the entries and she had no other option but to pick it herself.

She kept her hand on my upper thighs so close to my cock and pulled. She leaned down pressing her tits on the lower part of the thigh and picked up the pen.

My cock became too hard that I afraid it will push out of my trousers. Her tits felt heavenly.

I wished if she had kept it for more time. I looked at her face but it was unemotional.

Half an hour later I dropped my pen purposely between her legs.

I groped her thigh too high as my little finger was on the edge of her panties.

I bent down and my head touched her tits. I lifted the pen from the floor and raised my head rubbing her tits.

She said nothing and I was sure that she thought the act was unintentional.

The next day new stock came as the festive season was approaching.

Only both of us were in the go down to check the stock entries and attaching the price tags. No one will come until we finish our work.

This is the chance. I thought.

While attaching the price tags I brushed her thighs many times.

She may have thought that these were not deliberate touches and so she wasn't reacting.

I asked her to take an item for me. While she was picking up the shoe box I kept my hand on her thigh and squeezed gently.

"Unni, concentrate on your work." She said. To my surprise she wasn't angry. That gave me dare to try more.

I leaned closer to her face and blew some hot air from my mouth while my hand brushed her thigh.

"No." her voice was low. I saw her breast rising up and down faster.

I moved my hand closer to her sacred area while she was continuously listing the entries as I told her the batch number.

My hand was almost closer to her cunt, she made me stop.

"Unni, please don't."

I pulled my hands back but was now on her tits.

"Please, someone will see." She looked around.

"So you are worried about anyone seeing. If not, then it is okay for you." I shrugged.

She snickered in reply.

"No one will be coming. Even if anyone comes we will hear the footsteps before the person."

I was about to unbutton her shirt that we heard footsteps.

It was our boss' wife, Akhila.

"Hope you are not bored." She asked.

"No madam." Shreya replied.

"We are talking to each other and so we are good." I supported her.

"Everyone went to have lunch. I also came here to inform you that two more fresh stocks will be coming tomorrow."

"Okay madam." We shook our heads.

"I am going home now." she said and left.

Right after she left Shreya took my hand and kept it on her breasts. That was unexpected of her but I really liked her for taking the initiative.

I used both my hands and moved to her back to squash her melons. I unbuttoned her shirt and pressed her tits over her white bra.

My hard cock was touching her back. She gasped.

I made her stand and we went into a dark corner of the room.

I undone her jeans and inserted my fingers inside her panties.

I felt the heat of her cunt inside the panties. My rod was hard against her ass. I was kissing the nape of her neck as her hand dug inside her hair. She bent her head back and rested on my shoulder.

She took her hand behind her between our bodies and patted over my cock.

I pulled her panties down and my fingers trailed over her slit. One of my disobedient fingers entered the restricted area. I felt her moisture on my fingers. She was heated up.

She has already unzipped my jeans and took my rod out. She stroked it gently.

I was playing inside her cunt. My fingers went in and out in quick intervals. I heard her soft moans. Her sensual voices fired me up.

I removed her jeans and panties. She was completely naked down.

I stroked again inside her cunt while my other hand rubbed her clit.

She came in my hands. Still I didn't stop. "Oh yes, enough." She said.

She stood behind me now and stroked my cock. Her breasts were pressed against my back.

Her hand moved fast and my cock squirted out the cream.

We dressed up and started walking out when Indu showed up. "Aren't you guys going to have lunch?" she asked.

"We are coming." We said in a single voice.

Afternoon was uneventful but we enjoyed out time together.

She promised me to call in the evening.

She called me at 10.30 pm.

"Unni what are you doing?"

"I am at home thinking about you."

"Can you come here?"

"Now? Why?"

"Just come. I will tell you everything."

I knew this was an invitation. I wasn't going to refuse it.

"Give me a missed call when you reach."

I pushed my bike for almost 100 meters away from the house and started the engine.

I parked the bike in a plantation field little far from her house and walked under the shades.

I gave a missed call when I reached behind the house near the kitchen door.

I heard the door open and a soft voice of invitation. "Come in."

I went in. the whole world was under darkness.

A hand pulled me somewhere into the interiors of the house.

We stopped and I waited in the dark knowing nothing about what was happening.

The room was lit in an instant. I saw her standing naked in front of me.

"Ohh fuck."

It was the best ever sight to my eyes.

Shreya looked like a marble statue perfectly crafted.

My cock stood erect under my lungi making a tent in front of me.

"Where are the others?"

"They went to hospital as my uncle met with an accident."

"Why didn't you go?"

"Don't you remember what Akhila madam said? Two more stocks will arrive tomorrow."

"Are you going to sleep alone?"

"No. you are here to sleep with me."

She leaned onto me pressing her tits against my chest.

I wrapped my hands around her. My hard rod was knocking its head at her cunt lips looking for an entrance between her legs.

I lifted her head and sucked her red lips. I pushed my tongue into her mouth.

I felt her hand sliding down; she grabbed my cock and stroked it.

I groped her tits and started to crush them.

She kneeled before me after removing my lungi and throwing it to some corner of the room.

She mouthed my throbbing cock. She licked and sucked and nibbled my balls. I don't remember what all things she did with my cock. She was crazy.

"Uff... aah" I swirled in my position.

I made her stand up and kissed her tits. I sucked her nipples like a toddler.

I sucked down between her thighs slowly rising towards her cunt. I licked the slit and opened the cunt lips. Uff, the fragrance of her cunt entered my nostrils driving me wild.

I nibbled her clit as my hands clutched her from behind. Her ass got squeezed by my hands while her cunt lips were in my mouth.

My cock was jerking as it was signaling for action.

I took her to the bed. I climbed on top of her and rammed into her cunt.

"Aaaahhhh." She made a soft scream as she arched her back.

I pulled my cock out and then rammed into her again with more force.

"Aaaahhhhhh." She creamed louder.

I closed her mouth and started playing slowly. She moaned and gasped in low voices as I thrust into her continuously.

"How do you feel?" I asked.

"Fuck me, oh yes."

She hasn't heard what I asked. She was enjoying the sex.

I knew I was coming and took out before the lava burst out.

She understood that and took my cock in and I fucked her mouth.

Then it happened. My white lava came exploding into her mouth. She swallowed the whole cum without even wasting a single drop.

We were tired now. I wanted a seconds round but before that I thought a small rest would be better.

"You were so wild." I said. "Your husband?" I stopped in between.

"He left after a week of marriage. He didn't have much leave to stay back. I wasn't satisfied enough."

"Don't worry now I am here. I will satisfy you sexual needs." I said as I kissed her lips.

*****_____*****

******_______******